WELL DONE, MOMMY PENGUIN

CHRIS HAUGHTON

"Heaven is at the feet of mothers." —*Arabic saying*

For Mum

First US edition 2022

Library of Congress Catalog Card Number 2021953462
ISBN 978-1-5362-2865-6

22 23 24 25 26 27 CCP 10 9 8 7 6 5 4 3 2 1

Printed in Shenzhen, Guangdong, China

This book was typeset in SHH.
The illustrations were created digitally.

Candlewick Press
99 Dover Street
Somerville, Massachusetts 02144

www.candlewick.com

CANDLEWICK PRESS

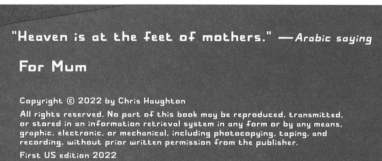

WELL DONE, MOMMY PENGUIN

CHRIS HAUGHTON

"OH! Where is Mommy going?" says Little Penguin.

"I think she's going to get dinner," says Daddy Penguin. "Come, let's take a look. Maybe we can see her."

"Can you see Mommy?"

"Yes, there she is! She's waving,"
cries Little Penguin.

All the penguins are trying to catch fish.
See them darting this way and that.

swoosh
swish
swoosh

She got it!

Well done,
Mommy Penguin.

"Mommy is good
at swimming,"
says Little Penguin.
"And she'll be back,
won't she?"

"She sure will,"
says Daddy Penguin.

They're coming
back already.
Look at them
leaping!

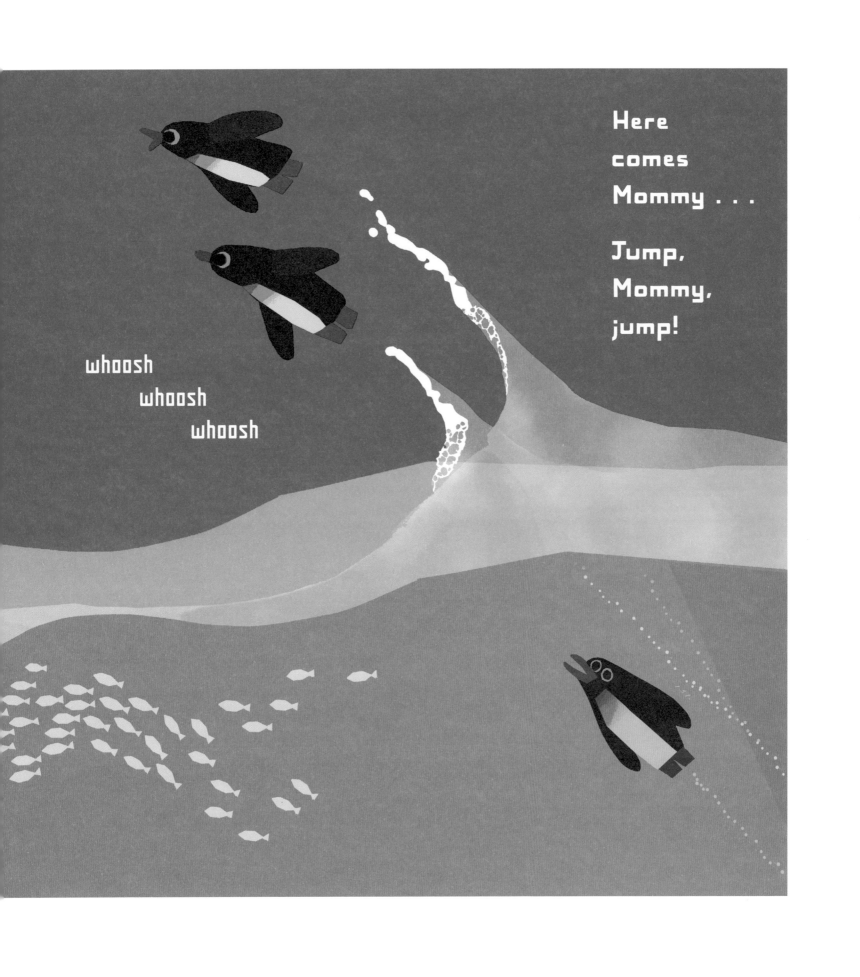

She made it!

Well done,
Mommy Penguin.

"Mommy is good
  at jumping,"
  says Little Penguin.
"And she'll be back soon,
  won't she?"

"She sure will,"
  says Daddy Penguin.

Now they are
climbing up the cliff.

cu-crunch
cu-crunch
cu-crunch

Here comes Mommy . . .

It's very slippy.
Be careful on
the ice, Mommy.

She did it!

Well done,
Mommy Penguin.

"Mommy is good at climbing,"
says Little Penguin.
"And she'll be here
very soon now,
won't she?"

"She sure will,"
says Daddy Penguin.

There's one last thing.
They have to sneak past
the sleeping seals . . .

Shh! Don't make
a sound.

tiptoe
    tiptoe
        tiptoe

It's Mommy's turn.
Be very quiet,
Mommy . . .

OH NO!

Mommy Penguin falls . . .

down
the
cliff ...

boink
boink
boink

Poor Mommy Penguin!
What's she going to do now?

Look, she's coming back!

Nothing's going to stop
Mommy Penguin.

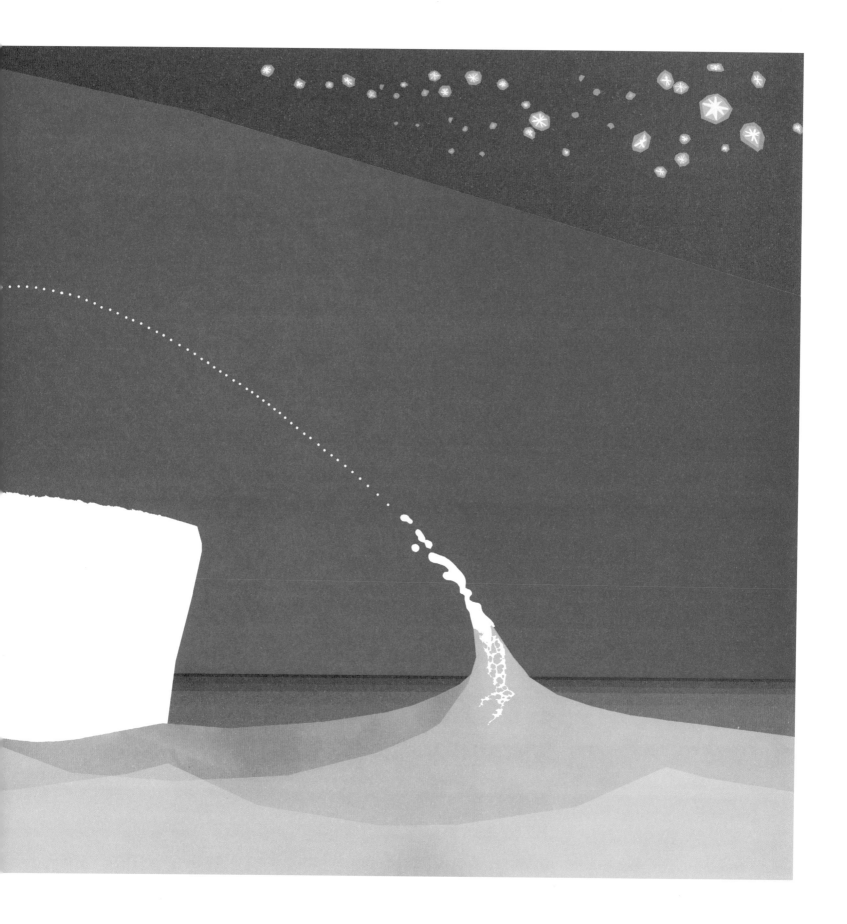

She leaps! She climbs!
She jumps over the seals!

Woo-hoo!

She's here!
She's HERE!

Well done,
Mommy Penguin.

And look what she's got . . .
DINNER!

"Mommy is the best," says Little Penguin.

"She sure is," says Daddy Penguin.

"Can I have some more?"
asks Little Penguin.